Put Your Teeth In Honey You're Not Dead Yet

by

SHARYN CHAPMAN

PUT YOUR TEETH IN HONEY YOU'RE NOT DEAD YET

The publisher does not have any control over and does not assume any responsibility for author or third-party websites or their content.

Cover art:
Copyright ©

Interior Images:
Copyright © Thinkstock/99815537/Heart/Hemera

Digital design by Telemachus Press, LLC
http://www.telemachuspress.com

Visit the author http://www.sharynchapman.com

Follow Sharyn Chapman on Twitter
https://twitter.com/#!/search/%40chapmanauthor

Visit Sharyn Chapman's Facebook Page
http://www.facebook.com/sharynchapmanauthor

ISBN# 978-1-939337-48-1 (eBook)
ISBN# 978-1-939337-49-8 (paperback)

Version 2013.05.03

Printed in the United States of America
10 9 8 7 6 5 4 3 2 1

TO MY HUSBAND DOUG

You Put A Song In My Heart

And Keep Laughter In My Soul

Also by Sharyn Chapman

Age With a Giggle was written to assist all women who are searching for a way to cope with aging and the plethora of woman's issues that we are faced with every day.

Women come in every size, shape and color and although we are paradoxically different, we are truly the same. Our experiences might change because of the zillion and twelve variables in our individual lives but our issues, feeling and desires remain constant.

See more at:

http://www.sharynchapman.com/Books.aspx#

Contents

Put Your Teeth In Honey
You're Not Dead Yet

A Funny Thing Happened On the Way to Maturity

Ah, the golden years, the final decades, the ultimate reward at the end of the rainbow. The carrot of utopia, that was promised to us if we just hung in long enough and tried hard enough is now within our grasp.

At age 65 the government officially affords us the title of senior. Since 1900 the percentage of Americans in this age group has more than tripled.

Today, this older population numbers in the millions, forty plus million at last count. We are now living longer thanks to modern medicine, better living conditions and *careful implementation of common sense.*

By now most of us have experienced years of happiness intertwined with loss, bad marriages, stressful jobs, sickness and an exhausting list of other problems, but the most important thing that we all can say is that *we are survivors!*

Destiny has led us to the *"some days of our dreams."* Haven't we all said "some day I will not have to get up and go to work, some day I will travel the world, some day I will skip to the grocery store without a care?" Well, I don't know about you but *I see a paltry few in this age group skipping anywhere.*

The enormous wrinkle in this *"successful survival story"* is our reward does not seem to be commensurate with our many years of thrashing to keep our heads above water.

Diseases we never knew existed lurk furtively around each corner. World issues lay onerously on our shoulders. Each morning is an adventure. What may have started small with an almost indiscernible muscle ache or slight stiffness might now represent itself as a mighty crescendo of painful joints, diminished hearing, poor digestion and high blood pressure.

Every day problems both emotional and physical can pile up like soiled laundry. Is this the reward we had in mind? Now, when we should be able to enjoy the bounty of our hard work and struggling we find ourselves instead **standing in long lines at the Pharmacy.**

New minefields and sky rocking health issues are what we are now being presented with when we are too tired and worn out from the battle. I always thought "old age" was going to be the **safety zone.** A time I could smugly look back on my life with reasonable satisfaction and start to reap the benefits. The question is now that I have paid my dues **are there any benefits to reap?**

Well negative thinking doesn't work. We have never given up before so why would we do so now? It is up to us to figure out how to put the glorious back into the glorious years, the gold back into the golden years, and **the kick back into our step even if our step is a bit slower?**

Aging Is Not Bad When
Compared To Tooth Extraction!

I am practical enough to know that life might now include more doctor appointments and other less desirable activities that unfortunately cannot be avoided, but along the way what is stopping us from noticing how brilliantly blue the sky is or how warm and delicious the sun feels on our possibly now *aching back?*

Actually bumps in the road can be a good thing. They are wake up calls that are meant to demand our attention. When these new challenges are presented to us, it is how we *think* about what is happening that will ultimately make the difference between *a satisfying life and one you might like to sell on EBay.*

What Sunshine Is To Flowers,
Smiles Are To Humanity.

Joseph Addison

Where Is Your Wisdom?

Think about the life you are now living. Does Monday's misery run into Tuesday's trouble? Is each day an undesirable, regurgitated copy of the last?

Day in and day out some find themselves following the same old patterns and dealing with the same old problems. So many of us have unknowingly jumped onto that bulging bandwagon with the rest of the **sad sorry seniors.**

Since the Grim Reaper has not knocked at your door yet, I respectfully suggest that you move away from that looming disaster and start to **live**. You might ask, how is this possible when I have health issues, money issues, family issues, etc., etc., etc. Well I am here to tell you that you can.

There is no magic wand that will remove any of our problems. Training ourselves to **view** these problems differently can diminish their value and return us to happiness sooner.

Stop the self persecution and adopt the attitude that whenever negativity comes our way we will dispense of it as quickly as we can and not allow it to live in the hollowed halls of our brains. *Remember, the irreverent brain cells that insist on going to the dark side will sap all of our energy.*

Dark Thoughts Produce Dark Habits. Dark Habits Result In An Unhappy Life.

According to People Facts, children laugh about 400 times a day, while adults laugh on average of 15 times a day. Well, that might be because life as a senior is not exactly laughable at times, but a keen sense of humor is almost as important as the air we breathe.

A smile will lighten your heart and show optimism the way in. It costs nothing to laugh and the benefits of doing so are countless.

The act of laughter brings more oxygen to your lungs, reduces stress levels and has a myriad of other great health advantages. ***An upbeat attitude trumps anything.*** Do not allow negativity to be elected as your state of mind.

Many of us have been programmed over our lifetimes to borrow problems before they even come to visit but being consumed with worry will make us old before our time.

If You Want To Know What Your Mind Was Like In The Past, Examine Your Body Now.

If You Want To Know What Your Life Will Be Like In The Future, Examine Your Mind Now.

Deepak Chopra

Positive thinking gives you the power of giants and negative thinking makes you weak and vulnerable. Stopping this daily assault is not that difficult. It is **all** about listening to what you are saying and making adjustments. Here is an example of what I am talking about.

"It's a beautiful day, I hope it doesn't rain later."

Do you realize the negative finish of that sentence just carelessly crushed the recognition of a beautiful day? Why not practice saying it more positively?

"It's a beautiful day and if it rains later, I won't have to go out and water my four petunias."

There are some obvious exceptions to this rule. For instance, if someone ran you over with a car I would **not** recommend that you to say, "How lovely this happened. Now I don't have to go home and wash the dog." In that case your positive attitude might initiate a nice long stay in the loony bin counting bingo cards.

In most cases positive thinking works miracles for both your physical and mental health. Many of our health issues are a product of decades of negative thinking. Why would we continue to let these negative thoughts and unhealthy actions rule our being? Isn't it time to break that cycle?

There is no nirvana but things will improve if you start showing life what you've got. Recapture your spirit. ***Recognize and celebrate the blessing you have been given and don't give power to anything else.***

Live in the moment. Once you push away all the bad thoughts you have more room for laughter. Show optimism the way in. Start focusing on the have's and let go of the have not's. ***Say good riddance to that doleful despondency you have been so exhaustingly carrying around.***

You're not dead so climb out of the casket and show the world that you know how to live. You know what makes you happy. Whether it is as small as turning off the ugly news on television or as big as running for president, do whatever it is that makes you complete. ***It is much nicer to keep life lit by the radiance of your smile and not to live in the darkness of a frown.***

There Is No Evidence To Date That
Life Is Meant To Be Serious.

George Burns

It's All Attitude Honey

When you wake up in the morning what are your first thoughts? Are you immediately consumed with all the problems in your life or do you give yourself a chance to feel blessed that you have been given another day? *I often wonder if somewhere in the heavens there are lines and lines of us anxiously waiting for angels to hand out our life expectancies, with the hope that we will make the most of the days we are given.*

Even though we all know we are very fortunate to be here, when life has given us a kick in the pants it is easy to say, "I quit. I am over this! I don't have the energy to fight any more battles or climb any more mountains."

When I feel like this I look to others for counsel and encouragement. *My own sweet aunt* is a survivor and a personal heroine to me. She has always been a wonderful example of how to live a happy and generous life.

She recently celebrated her 95th birthday. The adversities she has experienced in those 95 years could fill several lifetimes for others and she *still* manages to put a smile on her face most days.

Not only does she smile but also she will go to any length to make others smile and improve *their* day. She instinctively knows that this is her purpose and everyone who knows her will say she fulfills that purpose very well.

Why is she capable of this when others can barely pull themselves out of bed? *I believe it is because of her faith but also because she learned early in life that no one was going to make her life happy. It was a job she was here to do.*

She recognizes the gift each day is. Even when things do not go her way she thumbs her nose at problems and gets on with it. Is that always easy for her to do? Absolutely not!

Due to serious health problems she recently had to give up her home and move to a nursing facility. This was very disruptive and discouraging to her and for a short time I noticed her zest for life had somewhat diminished. At her significant age change is so much harder and she knew she had to muster everything she had in order to adjust to her new reality.

Last week when we spoke she said, "I can't talk long because I am decorating my room and then I'm going to meet a new friend."

Wow, I thought. Could I have rebounded from such a significant life happening as well and as quickly?

My aunt is a realist and knows the train is going down the track whether she wants it to or not. *She has made up her mind that it might not be train she wanted to be on but it is better than no train at all.*

Incidentally, she also told me that a much younger man (90 years young) was incredulous that she had recently celebrated her 95th birthday, *a comment that would make any girl's day!*

It is so easy to get down when life seems to be providing us nothing positive. We all, at times, feel like giving up the struggle but at some point clear thinking has to be regained. If you still have the ability to lift up your head and straighten your shoulders than why not do it? *Go to what is beautiful and restorative for you.*

Honor the age that you are and find contentment. You have survived what others may have not so give yourself a pat on the back and enjoy the day.

Remember, someone has to be an example to those behind you on the trail. Why not be the person they will think of with love and admiration and will hopefully learn from. Like my beautiful aunt, you will leave a legacy you can be proud of and *isn't that what life should be about?*

A Woman Is Like A Tea Bag You
Never Know How Strong It Is
Until It's In Hot Water.

Eleanor Roosevelt

To Age Or Not To Age, That Is The Question

Not exactly the quote from Shakespeare's lips but instead I have taken the liberty of adapting it to describe a subject people ponder profoundly. The subject is aging. Why do we do it? Can we avoid it? *Is it possible to enjoy it?*

According to a definition taken from Wikipedia, aging is the accumulation of changes in a person over time. In humans this includes three forms of change; physical, psychological and social.

There actually are a few advantages to growing older. Using a handicap parking space or not having to hold your stomach in can be real perks. The disadvantages however can outnumber the advantages if we are not careful.

They can include the slowing of our cognitive skills and declination of our general health with the Big Kahuna of disadvantages being that we ultimately die. *Really girls, who wants to do that?*

Certain countries and cultures boast about their records of longevity while others put forth a poorer showing. Roughly 100,000 people worldwide will die each day from things associated with old age and it seems that the country of Japan holds the record for the fewest of that number. Sushi anyone?

According to Huff Post World, Japan is reported to top the longevity charts with their male life expectancy at 79 and their female life expectancy at 86.1.

Italy comes in at number four with several other European countries also scoring well. Number twelve on the list is Canada and *finally the United States limps along behind at a pitiful 37.*

Why is the average life expectancy in the United States (men at only 75.6 and women at 80.8) lower than in these other countries? *Here, where we pay 2-5 times more for health coverage, we should smugly be sitting atop of the list.*

Also this **already disappointing number** will not be uniform for all U.S. citizens. In fact it has been found to be **lower yet** depending upon a persons heritage and geographic location.

No two people will age the same. Due to genetics, stress and increased risk of disease we all proceed through senescence (don't bother looking it up, it means aging) at our own rate.

As human beings we have spent centuries wondering if aging can be improved upon, slowed down or completely stopped. Diet change has recently been looked at as a way to add more years. Research has been done on calorie restriction and suggests that we take in 30-50 percent fewer calories than we would normally. As long as good nutrition is still had, calorie restriction has been shown to extend the lifespan of a mouse up to 50 percent.

Personally I would bet if the mice were given a choice, 9 out of 10 of them would rather have a field day with food and forget longevity. Until drug companies come up with a miracle pill, which will allow the user's body to mimic youth, we all will continue to age.

Here is something else to throw into the mix. Chronological age is very different than functional age. We all know chronological age is how many birthdays we can count but have you ever thought about your functional age?

As I drive to my doctor's appointment with dueling ailments I frequently pass sensational seniors busily biking along, defying their chronological age. Why is it that some of us seem to be able to stay active without a hiccup and others find the comfort of an easy chair more inviting and doable?

Baring an unsound body, a quote from that brainy Englishman Isaac Newton, says it all. "A body in motion stays in motion." If we continue to move our functional age will stay lower and our youth will last longer.

Now that we are at an age where pushing ourselves to be active might be as much fun and taking a bath with a toaster we still should **try to keep moving**, and **not** spend our days in our comfortable Barker lounger eating bon bons.

Sadly however, as much as we try to do all the right things, **longevity is not eternity.** We all give up the ghost sooner or later. The clock is ticking and unless you are on the forefront of the research and know something I don't know, my advice is to play the hand you are dealt and make the most of the life you have.

As you march down the road to Geezertown don't go with regrets tagging along behind as a constant reminder of a life not fully lived. Within reason, don't deprive yourself pleasure now for the sake of living an extra 30 minutes in a Nursing Home later.

Whatever is on your to do list, do. If the Professor on Gilligan's Island could make a radio out of a coconut you can make the best out of your day.

A Man Is Not Old Until Regrets Take The Place Of Dreams.

John Barrymore

From Diapers To Diapers

We only know what we know and by this point in our lives we should know a lot. But do we know everything? Not likely, and what we don't know **can** hurt us.

We are **dazzling damsels** all walking down the same path so why don't we feel comfortable discussing with each other what we are experiencing as we age?

Trusted friends, family and doctors are all at our disposal and can be looked to for a wealth of information but our pride, lack of confidence, or insecurity cause us to bottle up our concerns and pretend that they are not there.

Different stages of life may present new embarrassing moments and many of them can be mitigated or avoided. *What we perceive to be the unspeakable, the unmentionable, the private, the blush provoking happens to us all.*

21

Our bodies have gone through so much from childbearing to colonoscopies so by the time we have reached the state of sensational senior we **should** have learned how to move beyond embarrassment.

I realize our reluctance to talk about our problems can revert back to our upbringing or excessive propriety but really girls, at this point nothing should faze us.

Why spend multiple years unhappy or uncomfortable just because you do not have the courage to broach the subject and get advice.

Dale And Jack Were
Standing At The Bar

Dale Noticed Jack's Wife Moving
Her Feet Back And Forth Quickly

"Jack, Your Wife
Is Quite The Dancer"

Jack Smiled,
"She's Not Dancing, She's
Desperate For The Ladies Room."

Small mishaps as we age are the norm. ***Leakage spills and down the leg thrills can happen to us all.*** Things droop and drop until functionality is diminished. Mistaking Harold for Howard can be very embarrassing and don't pretend this has never happened to you. Millions of us hurriedly rush to buy products to alleviate these snafus and ***still*** we don't feel we can talk about them.

My wonderful friend, after an inordinate amount of years of my trying to engage her in conversation about her lack of hearing, finally revealed to me that she was ***thinking about*** going in to be fitted for a hearing aid. She was fraught with doubt. "Why," I asked.

"Well," she whispered quietly, "I don't want people to think I'm old."

Why so much drama? ***I wanted to tell her selecting a hearing device was not like going to buy a coffin.*** Instead, being the loving friend that I am I said,

"Good idea. Have you asked anyone for advice about this new acquisition? You know there are so many new kinds of hearing aids to choose from."

"Heck no," she whispered covertly. "Why would I want them to know what I was considering doing?" What would they think?

My answer should have been, They will think you can't hear but again, being the good friend that I am I simply said, "Be sure you get good advice from someone."

My friend is not alone in this thinking. So many of us live in fear of racking up another unpleasant milestone. I guess it is seen as one more step closer to the end of the proverbial road. But why? *Who cares what we need to get by as long as we do get by.*

We all should puff ourselves up like a sumo wrestler and project the confidence that we *hope we have* gained over the years. *Have the belief that nothing can bring you down.*

Make the changes that will facilitate life and when you don't know how to correct the problem on your own, for crimminy sake have the courage to ask someone else to help you muddle through.

Courage is contagious. You, baring your soul, will encourage others to do so as well.

Sometimes we forget that we are all here to help one another make this the best life possible.

As for men it can be different. They are not immune to embarrassment although I think they are for some reason they are better equipped to handle it.

When my husband was at a recent cocktail party the hostess said to him, "Oh my, I was so busy talking I forgot to put out the munchies," to which my husband answered, "You have monkeys?" Our strange looks made him realize his faux pas, he laughed and the following week simply made an appointment of his own.

What Is Success?

At Age 4 It's
Not Peeing In Your Pants.

At Age 94 It's
Not Peeing In Your Pants.

How Old Are You?
Really?

Remember when you were a teenager and you just could not wait to get into your 20's. Now instead of hoping to be older the concept of subtracting years is definitely more desirable.

There seems to be a universal wish by most seniors and that is to be able to go back and join the youth of our society as a permanent member. Well, honey, THAT ain't going to happen. It is what it is and all we have is the is. Wouldn't my English professor be proud of that sentence?

Age is only a number but sometimes it is a number we don't want to accept. The years used to tick off one by one at a slow and steady rate but as the senior segment of our lives approaches the years begin to speed by like a freight train out of control. ***Well, seriously girls, what can we do about it?***

Let's think about it this way. How old would we each be if we were not tagged with a number? I used to laugh at ladies who would refuse to give their age but I have reconsidered this point of view. I realize our body's general appearance and possibly reduced functionality can give a pretty good clue of the age we are but *you really are only as old as you think.*

If you walk around with the number of your years weighing heavily on you, how are you ever going to enjoy the scenery of your life?

George Burns said, "You can't help getting older but you don't have to get old." Good old George was a wise man.

Martha Graham danced until she was 76. Georgia O'Keefe painted well into her 90's. Colonel Sanders was ancient before he even thought about frying up some of that tasty chicken. *So why would you pack up and give up shop?*

Now unrealistic expectations are not going to do any of us any good. *We each have our own path to walk and some are definitely going up hill.* What I'm saying is in order to make the most of *your* day, use whatever resources *you* have to be happy.

Love yourself and treat yourself like you would treat a friend. You would never criticize or condemn a friend like you might be doing to yourself when you look into the mirror.

You are not obsolete and insignificant but valued and blessed. Let your sense of purpose change to reflect what now will make your life fulfilling and meaningful. *This* will open doors for you that you never thought existed.

Don't let aging victimize you. Stop and change what you can and then accept the rest. Be kind in your self-assessment and claim the age you feel in your heart and not the number.

A Light Heart Lives Longer.

William Shakespeare

One Night Around Midnight A Man Called His Doctor.

"I'm Sorry To Call So Late Doc," He Said "But I Think My Wife Has Appendicitis."

The Doctor Reminded Him As Graciously As He Could That He Had Removed His Wife's Appendix Five Years Ago.

"I Have Never Known A Woman To
Grow Another Appendix,"
Said The Doctor.

The Frantic Husband Said, "You
May Not Have Heard Of A Second
Appendix But You Must Have Heard
Of A Second Wife!"

Seriously, So Silly

No matter what our age, sometimes it's fun be lighthearted, silly and downright childish. I believe it keeps us young. When we observe the world around us we often can't believe the outrageousness we see and therefore can't help but chuckle.

Judging by the popularity of reality TV, it seems we really enjoy seeing others being vulnerable and love to be voyeurs while they make gargantuan mistakes that provoke us to say, *"Can you believe they just did that?"*

It is good for us to laugh at the bizarre, the unusual, the crazy and the inappropriate that we see all around us. Does that mean at this senior segment of our life that we are not acting maturely?

After a certain age we consider ourselves evolved and sophisticated and yet at times even when we are trying our hardest we still cannot keep a straight face and will laugh at the pain of others.

"Grow up." "No, you grow up." Like Peter Pan, we don't always want to grow up **because** when we do, certain things are expected of us.

We really **should not** laugh when strutting Sara slips off those three-inch heels she has no business wearing or when flighty Fred falls down the back stairs. **Why would** we laugh when someone could have become maimed or terribly hurt? Shouldn't what we choose to laugh about by this stage of life be more sensitive and responsible?

Laughter generally is in proportion to the act that produces it. If a person fell off of a six-story building I would hope the reaction of **most** people would **not** be to laugh. If they did they might rightly be considered a sociopath who should be driven directly to their personal psychiatrist. Watching someone simply trip over their own feet however, can be considered hysterical.

Different sexes process comical events differently. A man will often love the absurd and will laugh loud and long. *A women however generally has a more refined sense of humor and will employ sensitivity and a filter that men often lack.*

According to William F. Fry, a psychiatrist and laughter researcher at Stanford University, "Every human develops a sense of humor and everyone's taste is slightly different. But certain fundamental aspects of humor help explain why a misstep may elicit laughter."

When a person is faced with the unexpected or the ridiculously out of the norm, it is sometimes hard not to laugh. Falls are incongruent in the normal course of life in that they are unexpected. So despite our show of empathy we can still laugh.

For most of us this pattern of reaction is established early on. How many of us were plunked down in front of the television set by well meaning mothers to watch the Roadrunner use his cunning to lure in the Coyote and then blow him up? *Was this behavior mom was trying to instill in us?* Of course not, she saw it purely as entertainment and probably also as a moment of peace for herself.

I was one of those children and remember thinking that this was quite enjoyable. The more dramatic and sensational it was the more I seemed to enjoy it. But does being exposed to this at such an impressionable age set the stage of acceptance for cruelty and humiliation in later life or at least reduce our sensitivity to it? *Today, many of us program our VCR's so as not to miss certain programs that use a preposterous premise to be promised a preponderance of viewers.* If you have watched English television you will know what I am saying.

The English seem to have a healthy appreciation for anything silly and accident-prone. The whole slapstick industry has been built on our inability to restrain our laughter about the inane. The writers of America's Funniest Home Video's and Three Stooges are two examples that have capitalized on this concept brilliantly.

So now that we are at the *should know better* stage about anything we do in life are we then wrong to continue to enjoy what has given us pleasure and amusement?

I think as long as we are still able to discern the difference between sitcom silliness and responsible reality we should not deny ourselves the pleasure of watching. It's when we start patterning ourselves on their behavior that a re-examination of our moral fiber must happen.

I vote on behalf of a laugh any day. Making humor a significant part of our lives will trump the day-to-day situational seriousness that age dictates and will keep us young.

Age Is A Very
High Price For Maturity.

Who Is Eligible For Good Health, Raise Your Hand?

*A*bsolute good fortune is a lottery few of us win. With the advancement of years most of us have at least a few snippets of undesirable health come knocking at our door.

When the years accumulate we sometimes feel like we are carrying around a burden that is heavier than a pregnant elephant on an ice cream binge. The simple fact is aging can bestow terrible troubles on us all.

*For All We Know
We Don't Know A Thing.*

Good health is dependant upon many things. Even when lifestyle changes and nutritional intervention has been put in place and we follow all the "rules", rules that I might point out change on a daily basis, ***things can happen.***

What about all those sit ups I did, or the dozens of jogging shoes I wore out? Was all that effort for nothing you might ask? Well, the fact is that parts wear out, disease gets in and that well-oiled machine we once counted on might be leaving us stranded by the side of the road.

It starts with us noticing small changes and builds to the point where those pesky pains begin taking the upper hand and dictate very significant adjustments to how we must live. What used to be quick and easy can now present almost overwhelming challenges. What we did without aid might now require an arsenal of equipment.

Everything is different. How you move, how you feel, how you are forced to live in general. ***These adversities are not always easy to accept and overtime can make you angrier than a lion in diapers.***

We hearken back to the "good times" and then sadly realize we have a new reality. Daily life, instead of being relished and celebrated, might now be something we feel forced to accept and tolerate.

But—as I said in **AGE WITH A GIGGLE**, "we are all in the same slowly sinking boat *but* we are *not* taking on water yet." Don't allow yourself to be swept up into a tsunami of "D" words. Disappointment, despair and desperation are just a few of the emotions that are enemies to our happiness.

Come on girls, have you forgotten who you are? Have you ever before been the person who just threw in the towel and accepted things dictated to you? The strong chick you were is still there. Fly out of your nest and start ruling your universe.

Once you take the reins again you can design the day to go the way *you* want it to. *We can't change what we can't change but we can change a lot.* If we stop looking back to find what we have lost we will have more ability to recognize all that is good *now*.

The Beliefs Which Have Led You To Where You Are Today Are Not The Same As Those That Will Lead You Where You Wish To Go.

Albert Einstein

*Be Careful About
Reading Health Books
You May Die Of A Misprint!*

Mark Twain

My Teeth Don't
Live Here Anymore

Remember when you were a kid? Everything about you was new and wonderful including your teeth. If you did not take the best of care of them, *so what?* A new shiny set of them was soon to appear. *Besides wasn't losing teeth celebrated by a visit from the mysterious, money laden "tooth fairy?" Losing teeth was considered to be delightful adventure.*

Flash forward to senioritis. Missing teeth are now viewed in an entirely different way. Not only can it be unsightly but also lacking teeth can depreciate ones ability to chew and therefore *digest what we ingest on a daily basis.*

No one wants to sink their teeth into a juicy steak and have them stay there. My own husband spent a year reconstructing uncooperative teeth. During the process his ability to chew was diminished.

Knowing his nutrition could be at risk I began a campaign of pureeing anything known to man or beast so he could continue to eat and have proper nourishment. *At this point I believe I can make a delicious soup out of almost anything, including his left shoe.*

Good nutrition is paramount to us all so keeping those choppers healthy and present should be at the *top* of our responsibility list. It isn't all about just having a dazzling smile. Daily dental hygiene and regular visits to our dentist are now considered to be vital to *overall health*.

It is now said that inadequate dental care can also pave the way to heart disease. An article posted by The Mayo Clinic is quick to say, "Although poor oral health is not the *cause* of heart disease, it has been proven to contribute to such."

The new gets even scarier. "Bacteria on your teeth and gums could travel through your bloodstream and attach to fatty plaques in your arteries, making the plaques become more swollen (inflamed)." Did you know the human mouth has more than 700 different kinds of bacteria and you refuse to let your dog kiss *you?*

"If one of the plaques bursts and causes a blood clot to form, you can have a heart attack or stroke." *What? That's serious punishment for something as little as going to bed without brushing your teeth.*

The article continues to give us more good news. "It's possible that swelling in gums leads to swelling in other parts of your body, including your arteries. This swelling can *also* contribute to heart disease." Why do I do research about these things when it is so much more fun living in the land of denial?

With the products on the market today, we all have the ability to keep our precious assets around longer. Dentists assume the responsibility and perform heroics to save teeth whenever they can. When they determine the teeth can't be saved, they will provide a plethora of choices to meet our individual needs. ***Dentures, implants, pegs galore keep us smiling but somewhat poor.***

So what about the cost? Yikes. My friend says she has a Mercedes in her mouth! Imagine choosing between teeth and a new car? Fortunately I know she made the best choice, as her enjoyment of life would have been lessened without the shiny new teeth she has learned to love and P.S., she looks fabulous!

Some of us feel shame and a reduced sense of being when we don't look like those hot babes in the toothpaste commercials. ***Well honestly honey***, at this stage of life that might be not the only reason we don't look like them, but I digress. Food being prominently lodged between our possibly not so pearly whites or stuck in the gaping holes where teeth used to reside can be the reason we stop smiling.

Hearken back to photos of our ancestors and you will seldom see a smile. Not smiling makes us look unapproachable and aged. I recently met a woman who is in her 90's. Without even knowing her, my first impression was positive as she met everyone with a welcoming, sweet smile.

A Smile Is A Face Lift Without Surgery.

However you look at it, dental demise is something faced by us all and can be added to the list of "you laugh or you cry" items in life. Caring carefully for the *delightful dentitions* we are still blessed to have keeps us from winding up with a staring role on "Tooth or Consequences."

A Woman And Her Husband Went To The Dentist

"I Want A Tooth Pulled And I Don't Want Novocain Because I'm In A Hurry," The Woman Said

"Just Extract The Tooth As Quickly As Possible, And We Will Be On Our Way"

The Dentist Was Quite Impressed "You Are Really Courageous," He Said. "Which Tooth Is It?"

The Woman Turned To Her Husband And Said, "Open Your Mouth, Dear."

Tooting Your Own Horn

I have heard the "tongue in cheek" statement that to have permission by society to fart in the open could help to take the stress out of everyday life. Having said that, I would like to go on the record saying that I consider myself reasonably proper and therefore do not condone this practice or use the word.

I have to admit however, using other softened and somewhat more courteous sounding substitutions for **the word** might give less importance to **the act** than it deserves. The healthy human body will pass wind 15-25 times a day producing around a half liter of gas. Heck, people even do it while they are asleep.

As a person ages and a digestive system becomes less efficient, this emission might become even more frequent. So, if we all do it all the time why do we make such a big deal about it? According to an article published in 2009 by Alistair Briggs, Emperor Claudius of the Roman Empire many moons ago decreed this public emitting of gas accompanied by sounds and possibly unpleasant odors, **legal at banquets**, stating it was for the good health of the people.

It's Scary When You Start Making The Same Noises As Your Coffee Maker.

Actually, I hesitate to think what it **would** be like if we all were not able to expel quietly at will. The human body could become a flotation device and therefore require tethering or weights to keep us all from drifting away in a breeze.

Also, can you imagine how uncomfortable it would be? Containment of this flatulence would take heroic strength and can you imagine **if** a leak then **did** occur?

I guess it depends upon how you may have been raised. *The prim and proper of us would rather be known for kicking a puppy down a flight of stairs than ever letting a sound slip publically from our posterior.*

But some of us feel differently. Recently, I was in a big box store, ironically shopping for toilet tissue. The aisles were congested and I found myself walking behind a very attractive, well-dressed elderly man.

As we all snailed along toward our individual destinations I began to hear something that sounded like a popgun going off.

I looked around and saw nothing out of order so continued on my way. As someone up front slowed our passage even more, I then found myself directly beside the gentleman. *Suddenly the sound happened again, this time more clearly definable* and for a *longer duration*.

Our eyes met and he smiled at me in a lovely way. Of course, I smiled back. I had solved the mystery, backed up quickly and turned down another aisle. He on the other hand continued on with a very contented, **stress free** look on his face. I was torn between convulsing in laughter and admiration.

I was aware that as proper and pleasant as he was, he was not going to be governed by **societies rules**. So the question is does age lessen our ability to refrain or does age give us permission not be bother to contain?

My grandson said the elderly janitor at his school makes a hissing sound when he bends over and asked me what I thought it was. My answer to him was that some sounds shouldn't be investigated but might smartly be avoided.

So do we want to live in a world where everyone is comfortable openly creating this kind of music? Personally, I happen to like things the way they are.

Dale Was A Farmer
In Montana Who Was In Need
Of A New Milk Cow.

He Heard About One That Was A
Real Deal In North Dakota.

He Drove Over And Gave The Cow
A Try. Each Time He Grabbed
Her Teat She Would Fart.

He Thought This Was Unusual
But As The Price Was Right
He Paid The Man And
Brought The Cow Home.

The Next Day He Asked
His Neighbor Tom To Come

And See His New Cow.
Dale Said, "Sit Down
And Milk Her, Tom."

Tom Sat Down And Gave A Good
Pull. When He Did Of Course
The Cow Farted.

Unfazed Tom Said, "You Bought
This Cow In North Dakota."

Dale Was Shocked.
"How Did You Know
Where She Came From?"
He Asked.

Tom Said, "My Wife
Is From North Dakota."

My Photographic Memory Is Out Of Film

"**H**ey honey, I found my keys. They were in the fridge. I told you they would show up sooner or later." Does this sound familiar? Millions of us find ourselves asking the question, where did I put this and why did I do that?

The lack of cognitive ability and loss of memory is a common complaint of many members of the senior set. Names and dates once vaulted away seem to have evaporated. Where did they go? *What was on the tip of our tongues is just gone.* We still have a lot on the ball but have we forgotten how to bounce it?

Over our lives our bank account of knowledge grows and deepens and that gelatinous gray matter between our ears does an admirable job of keeping up with and properly categorizing the incoming information.

At some point however this highly productive unit starts to slow up and we fear the possibility of a complete shut down. This total cooperation we once enjoyed and may have taken for granted for so much of our lives now presents ***a new reason for us to practice patience.***

Most of the time memory loss is a routine slowing of our brain process and should not be considered a worry. Frequently when we fret over something we expected to be immediately available it will show up on a later train, possibly arriving in the middle of the night.

A Clear Conscience Can Be The Sign Of Bad Memory.

The mind has a mind of it's own and demands to be worked out. After a certain age it is *expected* that the brain process will languish if it is not challenged. Keeping the mind active will allow it to keep growing and therefore prosper.

I am personally taking Spanish lessons. Convincing the vocabulary to stay in my brain is like trying to persuade jelly to stay stapled to the ceiling. My constant practicing of vocabulary that drives everyone around me insane still leaves me with a very limited ability to converse with my friend Jose.

Moving our bodies is also very good for the brain. Exercise in any form is beneficial and just plain old walking is a great friend of a sound memory. Moving even at a slow pace lessons your stress and increases the blood flow that is so necessary for a robust brain.

So if your doctor is on board, **Simon Says** put on your cute little jogging suit and take your show-stopping smile for a walk. Start slow and build up. Moving keeps you grooving!

Research tells us that those who walk 6-9 miles a week can prevent brain shrinkage and cut their risk of developing memory loss in half. ***Doing this while observing nature or*** *checking out the new muscle bound gardener down the street might turn into the best part of your day!*

Other activities are also valuable for brain health. Starting a new project around the house, learning new games like Bridge, crafting, reading, or researching how the *rare tree kangaroo* got it's name are just a few activities that will keep our exceptional intellectual abilities intact.

My Mind Wanders And Sometimes Leaves Me Completely.

It goes without saying that staying that optimum *general health* is vital to mind preservation and this should include eating lots of fruits and vegetables and omega 3 fats. Doing this on a regular basis is not a guarantee your brain will not get rusty but will put you on the *plus side of hopeful*.

Getting enough sleep and reducing stress are two other big factors that can't be ignored. Not sleeping well imbalances hormones and we all know what havoc *those little devils* can

raise when they are not happy.

Many medications such as sleeping pills, painkillers, and anti-anxiety pills could possibly impact your brain. Depression, excessive smoking and over consumption of alcohol also can mimic memory loss.

It is always best to stay in contact with your doctor and let his advice guide your way. It's the old "monkey off your back" thing. Once you hand your troubles over to someone else your burden will be lighter and your day should be brighter.

Two Elderly Ladies Had Been
Friends For Many Decades. Over
The Years, They Would Meet
Every Tuesday To Play Cards

One Day One Looked At The
Other And Said, "Now Don't Get
Mad At Me But I Just Can't
Think Of Your Name.
Please Tell Me What It Is"

Her Friend Glared At Her
For At Least Three Minutes
And Then Said, "How Soon
Do You Need To Know?"

Meet The Bickersons

Marriage *can be* defined as the state where one person is right and the other person is a husband. But to be fair, this legal merging of hearts is actually viewed by most as a lifetime promise of utopia and is the ultimate goal of many love-struck girls.

With romance in our hearts we go forward into what we perceive will be the promise of happiness. Many of us reading this consider that to be true and others have just had our stomachs turn having experienced the worst the institution has had to offer. *If marriage is so fallible then why do we tumble into this perilous pit that offers no guarantees.*

Red Skelton has offered an interesting viewpoint about his marriage. To keep it fresh he recommends sleeping in separate beds. Hers is in California and his is in Texas!

Seriously girls, the tree of marriage has to be fed with loving comments and mutual respect. Taking on the habit of nipping at each other's heels about *everything* will lead us to the bank of bad choices and making a withdrawal there can have devastating consequences.

My Husband And I Divorced Over Religious Differences,

He Thought He Was God And I Didn't.

Lady Astor once said to Churchill, "If you were my husband, I'd give you poison." Not to be undone Churchill replied, "If you were my wife, I'd take it."

Respect, patience and mutual participation from both participants is required to sustain a good relationship. We assume our roles, dictated by society, and hope the other person will hold up their end of the bargain.

When we slack even in the smallest way **skirmishes or harsh words can ensue**. Asking for any assistance from **some** men can be the most frustrating part of your day.

"Jack will you take out the trash please?" An hour later, "Jack did you take out the trash?" An hour later, "Jack what about this trash that I have asked you twice before to take out!" Finally the trash is removed accompanied by a sour face and incoherent mumbling.

When we sign on the dotted line and march down the aisle with gleeful expectations we are never quite sure which way it will go. *Life can give us many years of bliss or turn a couple of innocent young people into the Bickersons who ultimately get tired of the skirmishing and rush to undo what has been done.*

Marriage Is The Number One Cause Of Divorce.

Red Skelton

The divorce rate in 2013 in America is hovering around 50%. *That means half of all who have walked this way together have turned around and walked back alone.*

There are innumerable reasons that we can ultimately sign up for the dreaded dissolution of our marriage. Regardless of the reason we are often left feeling empty and alone. Even the women for whom a marriage works can have tragedy strike and find themselves widowed and wondering what the rest of her life will be like.

By the time we are seniors this love we derived from a relationship and might have taken for granted at the time is even a greater loss. Now when we need the comfort that love gives more than ever we might find ourselves without.

The good new is that there are many kinds of love and many people waiting to give and received it. The majority of us would choose to have companionship in **whatever** form it comes. Taking another jaunt down the aisle or even tying the knot on the courthouse steps can certainly starve off loneliness, although it is said a woman over 40 has more of a chance of **being killed by a terrorist** than finding the right man to jaunt with.

In Our Older Years We Can Continue To Chase Women But Now Only When They Are Going Down Hill.

Bob Hope

Companionship can also be found in a wonderful friendship. Love will blanket you when you give of yourself through volunteerism or just reach out to those in need. And don't forget, it can also be derived from a **warm puppy** even when it keeps you up at night.

If you have lost who you had deemed to be your soul mate or life companion don't allow the experience to write the rest of your story. Dr. Phil says, "Sometimes you just have to give yourself what you wish someone else would give you."

We all just want a hand to hold and a heart to listen to. For every lonely person with a broken heart there is at least one other person ready to reach out and help. Make it your priority to go out and find that person and share your love. Be the ear that listens and the heart that cares. *Remember any love you give away comes back times two and will reward you greatly.*

A Couple Drove Down A Country
Road For Several Miles, Not
Saying A Word.

An Earlier Discussion Had Led To
An Argument And Neither
Of Them Wanted To
Concede Their Position.

As They Passed A Barnyard Of
Mules, Jack Asses And Pigs,
The Husband Asked Sarcastically,
"Relatives Of Yours?"

"Yep," The Wife Replied, "In-Laws."

Sex And The Senior Girl

How many times have your heard someone say, "I don't know what I do all day but it takes me all day to do it." Over the years our well-honed multitasking skills have slowly been downgraded to significantly slower single tasking. What we did in a morning **then** can easily take the whole day **now**.

Everything can require more of an effort, even sex. Now listen carefully girls. *I did not say that senior sex wasn't enjoyable but in this case the word enjoyable might need to be slightly redefined.*

One Day, A Man Came Home And Was Greeted By His Wife Dressed In A Very Sexy Nightie.

"Tie Me Up," She Purred, "And You Can Do Anything You Want."

So—He Tied Her Up And Went Golfing.

In the early years lovemaking was fantastic, fresh, furious. It was spontaneous and never undesirable. It was as if our bodies were preprogrammed to listen to the melody of our hormones and then comply with ease.

Now that your girlish figure might be gone and your body has adjusted to an advanced maturity, a roll in the hay might be considered to be as pleasurable as getting your finger caught in a screen door.

Diminishment of the sex drive is a natural phenomenon that will affect a good portion of the senior population however there is little doubt that **some seniors** are still rocking it. It seems all it requires is two willing participants, a little desire and possibly **a small blue pill**.

Certain medications like high blood pressure drugs and pills taken for depression can lower ones libido and that in turn reduces ones ability to perform. Not to let us down the pharmaceutical industry has successfully developed a whole host of new medications that are readily available. **These miracle pills keep those randy rascals ready and are selling like hot cakes.** Now, if we are healthy and interested, with the aid of these medications we can be sexual beings until we step into our grave!

Being alone and lonely encourages many of us to move forward using what is at our disposal to meet a new companion or a future mate. **Online dating has gone far to change revered elders into starry-eyed hopefuls who hop in and out of bed while hoping and praying not to pop a hip in the process.**

Throwing your hat back into the ring **can come** with a couple of significant side effects. While wandering wistfully into this wonderland one must be aware of the possibility of contracting any number of Sexually Transmitted Diseases.

Sister Mary Told Sister Anne That One Of The Other Nuns Had Gotten A Case Of Chlamydia.

Sister Anne Said, "That's Great, I Was Getting Tired Of Chardonnay."

A Centers for Disease Control and Prevention report states that many single women, nearly 60 percent, that were sexually active did not consider it necessary to require a condom. The fact is most women considered STDs and HIV **prostitute diseases** and seeing they had no concern about becoming pregnant, they saw no need to protect themselves.

If you are in the group that thinks sex **now** is over-rated and a **nooner** represents a nap, then consider yourself fairly normal. ***There are plenty of other ways to amuse yourself.*** If you are in the group that thinks a romp in the **geriatric jungle** with your undies hanging off of your ankle might put the cherry on your senior sundae, then good for you but for your sake and the sake of others, **use protection**.

Live Your Life And Forget Your Age.

Norman Vincent Peale

Nothing will compare to the choices we all had when we were young but don't forget that 60 is sexy. Seventy is sensational. ***Each decade you get more and more fantastic and as long as you believe that, you will own your world.***

When I Am Good, I'm Very Good,
But When I'm Bad I'm Better.

Mae West

Tired Of A Listless Sex Life, The Man Came Right Out And Asked His Wife During A Recent Lovemaking Session,

"How Come You Never Tell Me When You Have An Orgasm?"

She Glanced At Him Casually And Replied, "You're Never Home!"

A Man goes To A
Shrink And Says,

"Doctor, My Wife Is Unfaithful
To Me. Every Evening She Goes To
Larry's Bar And Picks Up Men.

In Fact, She Sleeps With Anybody
Who Asks Her! What Do You
Think I Should Do?"

"Relax," Said The Doctor, "Take A
Deep Breath And Calm Down.

Now Tell Me Exactly Where Is
This Larry's Bar?"

Controlling Our World

"**P**ut your hand on a hot stove for a minute and it seems like an hour. Sit with a pretty girl for an hour and it seems like a minute." According to Albert Einstein, that defines relativity.

Time flies when you're having fun but guess what, time flies also when fun is absent. Depending upon how you look at it, the ticking clock keeps moving and can be considered our enemy. Making the most of your day, everyday is the only answer.

Agonizing over what you have lost will not allow you to appreciate all that you have gained. *William James said, "How pleasant is the day when we give up striving to be young or slender."* Desperately holding on to old and stale ideas allows no room for fresh new ones. Knowing that change can be difficult for some and impossible for others how do we preserve our happiness?

I was at the grocery store last week and the young whippersnapper bagging my purchases asked in an accusatory tone, "Didn't you bring your reusable bags?" Well, I intended to but I was in a hurry and just forgot. With disgust in his voice he then said "paper or plastic?"

Now, I think the policy of bringing reusable bags is a terrific one. No one can deny that we are jamming our landfills with materials that will outlive you, me, and the Christmas Grinch but this young man's haughty attitude riled me up.

I thought about his question for a moment and in a clear voice said, "I am bi-saxual, you make the choice." The cashier, being of my ilk was killing herself not to laugh. The groceries remained unpacked on the counter as the young man froze upon receipt of my words. I finally gave him one of my best smiles to put him out of his misery and began to pack the groceries myself. I tell this story for a few reasons.

The world is changing every moment of every day and if we don't want to be left behind we have to make a strong effort to stay on board. Hence, following the rules that might ultimately save our planet is a good idea.

New rules, new practices, new ways of thinking might be harder to swallow than pocketful of peas but after carefully processing them, be open minded to at least give acceptance to what you feel you can live with and a wide berth to those you feel can not.

As the waistline expands the list of what we find tolerable can shrink. Last Christmas my husband over heard me placing a telephone order for a menorah. Honey, he said, are you changing religions this year? Why on earth do we need a menorah?

Don't be silly I said. I would like to demonstrate religious tolerance to our grandkids and this will be a perfect way. *Having a menorah in our living room doesn't make me a Jew anymore than standing in a garage makes me a car!*

It was a small act that delivered a loud message. *It doesn't matter if you are of the dreidel, cradle, or any number of other persuasions, tolerance, peace and forgiveness should be the goal for us all.* We might have to change many things but should not change the important, vital person we are. We could be as old as Methuselah but we still have value. So with humor and grace we should never let anyone make us feel ancient, unimportant or out of touch.

All the people of your past will not fit into your future. Some people lift you up and give your dreams wings. Others keep you down and won't allow you to fly. You are too fabulous to allow this to happen.

You will never succeed with one foot glued to the ground and your head in the sand. The only way of finding peace is to open our minds and reach for acceptance. Eliminate all toxic thoughts with a giant eraser. Don't let your emotions make decisions for you. *Even if you are so angry with someone that you would take pleasure in seeing him eat his own liver, practice forgiveness. Know this, teach this, and incorporate this in how you live the rest of your life.*

Another good place to do this is within the family. The possible pitfalls of parenting are plentiful and for centuries have caused great strife in families. Mending the messes we make won't happen overnight but why the holly halleluiah wouldn't we try. We might fail but God is not counting our tears so don't be afraid to shed a few.

Fighting can become nothing more than an unpleasant habit. None of us has to win every argument. *The real art of conversation is not only to say the right thing at the right time, but also to leave unsaid the wrong thing at any time.*

George Burns said, "The secret of a good fight is to have a good beginning and a good ending and to have the two as close together as possible." I could not have said it better.

Have faith in mankind. *Lack of trust will cause a relationship of any kind to wilt like a late summer flower.* Anger is only one letter short of danger. Agree to disagree. Make peace with the past in order to enjoy the future. Think about how proud you will be if you succeed.

An old Colombian proverb says, "*With patience and saliva the ant swallows the elephant.*" The playing ground is different but we all are still in the game. Enjoy your life, the most wonderful gift you have ever been given, to the end.

One Evening An Old Cherokee Man Told His Grandson About The Battle That Goes On Inside People.

He Said, "My Son, The Battle Is Between Two Wolves. One Is Called Evil And It Is Filled With Anger, Envy, Jealousy, Sorrow, Regret, Greed, Arrogance, Self-Pity, Guilt, Resentment, Inferiority, Lies, False Pride, Superiority And Ego.

The Other Wolf's Name Is Good And It is Filled With Joy, Peace,

Love, Hope, Serenity, Humility,
Kindness, Benevolence, Empathy,
Generosity, Truth, Compassion
And Faith."

The Grandson Thought About
It For A Minute And Then
Asked His Grandfather, "
Which Wolf Wins?"

The Old Cherokee Simply Replied,
"The One You Feed."

Being Grateful
It's A Good Thing

Being grateful is one of the first lessons we teach our kids but this lesson can be forgotten by us as we face life as a senior. A beautiful butterfly briefly landing on our shoulder, finding an available parking place close to our destination and a long overdue phone call from a loved one are just some of the many things we should be grateful for. Have we forgotten how to recognize their value? ***Have we gotten so hardened by the world around us that we don't even notice what is there?***

You creek, you grunt, you even groan but guess what ladies you're not alone. Millions of people get up feeling like that every day. If this is your life you might say, "why should I be grateful?" Studies have shown that there are a myriad of reasons to show gratitude and if you take the blinders off, you too will see that they do exist. For every one thing on your plate of worries there is a counterbalance of good.

Any one of us can make a mountain out of a molehill by just adding dirt but remember worry is interest paid on trouble before it happens. Why do we do this?

"I am miserable with this cold but I am so fortunate that it is not pneumonia."

You could have stopped that sentence at the word cold and left yourself feeling down, but finishing it with the optimistic thought keeps you sustained.

Some People Are Always Grumbling Because Roses Have Thorns I Am Thankful That Thorns Have Roses.

Alphonse Karr

This thinking might not come naturally to you at first and might require some serious work to break what I call *"negative navigation through life."* Many of us have worked diligently to feed this negativity so starving it off will take some awareness and effort.

Research has found that the most content are those who can break the noose hold the negative thoughts have on us and move on as soon as possible.

No One Gets Everything And No One Gets Nothing.

Laughing at life and being grateful is valuable but what about when life doesn't allow you to laugh? There are moments when what is happening is *just too serious*. Turn on the news and you will hear things that will make you want to go back to bed and stay there indefinitely but every so often they will treat us to a soul enriching story about someone who has had *great tragedy* and still has found the strength in their inner being to be grateful.

Hardballs can come at any of us and sometimes all you can do is lick your wounds and feel a little sorry for yourself. But—don't be the envelope no one wants to open. *Once you know your shoes match stop looking down.* Keep your eyes and your attitude up. Even in the direst of circumstances, there is always something to be grateful for.

We all have and we all lack. Train yourself to make the best of what you *have* even when *lack* is smacking you upside the head. You might not have the lightheartedness of a teenager but life is what you make it to be and after an appropriate amount of time choose the good feelings and don't allow yourself to wallow in what has hurt you.

Life is a bumpy road which forces us to hang on tight but that pot of gold, although possibly a little more tarnished, is still there. ***Blessed are those who can give without remembering and receive without forgetting.***

I Was Talking With A Woman At A Club Last Night. She Looked Pretty Good For A 60 Year Old.

I Found Myself Thinking
How Grateful I Was
That I Had Met Her
As She Probably Has A Really
Hot Daughter That I Could Meet.

After We Drank For A While She Said, "Would You Like To Come Home With Me For A Threesome."

What The Heck.
If She Looked This Good
Her Daughter Has To Be
Amazing.

I Was Excited By The Time We
Arrived At Her Place, She Opened
The Door And Shouted Upstairs,

"I Brought Someone Home Mom,
Are You Ready?"

Share What's Between Your Ears

Who cares what I know. I'm old as dirt and don't have anything to offer anyone. How could I possibly enrich a young person's life by mentoring? Well I am here to answer that question for you in two simple words. ***You can.***

Even if you did not run IBM or contribute to the launching of a space satellite, whether you realize it or not, you have lived a life of knowledge gathering and after chipping out what you have learned to be important now it is time to pass this valuable largess along. Why would you ***not*** share this information with the younger ranks?

The Best Classroom Is At The Feet Of An Elderly Person.

Andy Rooney

In the high-speed, broken family, confusing world we live in how many of us will take the time to mentor? You can start in your own family, regaling them with stories that have moral messages and those which will teach lessons.

Those you have hogtied to listen might resist at first but be diligent. Continue to take every opportunity you get to slip in valuable bits of information that will provoke them think and that will add value to their lives.

Initiate discussions regarding current events and demonstrate to young people how it is so very important to use their own minds, be balanced in their thinking and fair in their judgments rather than sheeping along with thoughts and actions of their contemporaries.

Along with this, instead of spending your day *feeding that living organism of depression*, volunteer at a school to read to little ones or to share whatever skill you have. Spread fertilizer on any young mind and it will grow and flourish. Being gently persistent over a period of time might one day surprise you with a positive result from the toughest of audiences.

Not everything that counts can be counted. You might think performing these acts is *nothing in the scheme of things* but to others it can be everything. No only does this occasionally relieve the everyday responsibilities of our parents and or teachers but gives the kids a special treat to look forward to. A special treat that would be missed. Wouldn't that be a nice way to think about yourself?

Knowing all those young minds were counting on you has to lift your spirits and give you a purpose. *Trying something new is a wonderful exercise for the brain or would you rather sit around and argue with Alzheimer's?*

Don't squander your day in a rut that you have so copiously and carefully prepared. We all know that rut dwelling takes a toll on our happiness. Climb out and see what you can offer the world. It is important to enjoy old memories but just as important to keep making new ones.

Spend your most precious time leaving footprints on the mind and souls of angels. Doing this will not allow you time to feed any unhealthy thoughts that were bogging you down and keeping you from living your best life.

Whether You Think You Can Or You Think You Can't You're Right.

Henry Ford

Open Mouth, Insert Foot

An old Yiddish proverb says, "The wise man, even when he holds his tongue, says more than the fool when he speaks."

The happiness in your life is dependant upon the quality of your thoughts and words. Are they always pure? Are they always right? ***Should they always be spoken?***

When life goes in a direction that *you* might not have chosen some of us might over react and say things that we wish we hadn't. Sometimes it is very difficult **not** to speak out when the world is throwing you curves and your belief system is being challenged.

When your son comes home and introduces you to the girl of his dreams and all you see is makeup and miniskirts it is very hard to be kind with your comments and many of us will react and then regret.

Sometimes words can hurt more than actions. They come tumbling out of our mouths like lava from a volcano destroying anything in their path and once it's said, it will **never** be forgotten. Choosing our words carefully or **momentarily stepping back** from a situation until it can be assessed properly can save us all from embarrassment and possibly egg on our face.

This practice can be even more important when advising grandchildren. These priceless assets are the breath of fresh air that we are blessed to receive after our long journey of living life. We adore them for **a zillion and twelve reasons** and want the best for them.

It is a gift to love them and our responsibility to guide them but it is vital that **we do not step on the toes of the parents** from whom they have been born. Filling grandkids heads with what may be contrary to the parent's teachings might drive a shiv between you all and **that makes no one happy**. Boundaries, girls boundaries.

I remember back in the dark ages when doctors made house calls. My own professional practitioner would arrive spewing smoke in every direction. Back then, smoking was not known for carcinogens but was considered medically sound and probably thought to be "cool." I remember him suggesting to my mom that it might help her manage anxiety! Would we pass this on as valued information today? Goodness no!

What Was Considered To Be Valuable Advice From Our Era Could Be Tantamount To Child Abuse Now.

Harry S. Truman said, "I have found that the best way to give advice to my children is to find out what they want to do and advise them to do it." *I am very confident this would not apply to decisions that would affect the safety or emotional well being of the child but would be more about the philosophy and choices regarding the child's rearing.*

Love your little ones and be the best grandparent you can be but for a happy family leave the parenting to the parents. *Honestly girls, keeping your wallet open and your mouth closed might be the best advice of all.*

That could be true in innumerable other situations as well. Even when you have to bite the inside of your mouth until it bleeds, to live harmoniously and happily it is so vital that we not burn the bridge that we might want to walk over again.

A Son Called His Mom And Asked How She Was

"Not Too Good," Said The Mother, "I Haven't Eaten For 38 Days."

"That's Terrible," The Son Said, "Why Would You Do That?"

The Mother Smiled To Herself And Said, "Because I Didn't Want My Mouth To Be Full In Case You Should Call."

Tell Them
You Love Them, Stupid

As we age, change comes in innumerable varieties. It can be in your health, your life style, your relationships, your marital status, your financial status, your appearance, blah, blah, blah. The list goes on and on.

How we adjust to the changes varies *greatly* from person to person but for many of us, when the changes are *not* voluntary, our emotions can drop down deeper than a baritone performing a sullen opera.

Many of these changes we experience are quite impactful. Some will demonstrate our personal growth over the years and some will put a beacon on our failures. Like it or not, you are on the clock. This is the time we are offered to kill or cure all that ails us.

But the good news is that years of experiences, both happy and sad will always teach us *if we are paying attention* and can pave our way to what hopefully will be better decision-making and more happiness.

Would you ever now think that it is supremely important to be so skinny that you might slip through a sewer grate? Changing our thinking as we mature is paramount. Nothing petty, trivial or sophomoric ***should be*** given space in our minds but yet ***unless we have lived a solitary life on the Serengeti***, some of us have had experiences that are hard to forget and we will persist in holding on to bad feelings and the anger that results. Even as simple as finding themselves being directed by others who really can't know ***their heart's desire*** can ruin a day.

"What in the world are you wearing?" one sister said to another. "You look terrible in red!"

How many of us would run back to our closets and change or dissolve into tears? After all these years of living and breathing we still can be crushed and possibly manipulated by a comment like this. ***But why should we?***

Today, make your mind up to be the contractor of your own life. This is the day you can *move forward* and begin to design what will be tomorrow's miracle. Henry David Thoreau said it best when he uttered, "Never look back unless you're planning to go that way."

People have diligently fought wars for centuries and when asked *why,* they might not have a clue. What long ago was considered to be supremely important may have had it's importance usurped by time.

This is so true of grudges. We might not even remember what initiated them and yet many of us may have diligently continued to give them power for decades. Anger and bitterness will hurt *you* the most. *How we thought then is not how we should think now!*

Bundle up all your regrets, grudges and old resentments and while you are at it you might as well include your useless worry. *Tie them all up tighter than a mini van filled with monkeys and then ceremonially discard them like the worthless rubbish they are.*

Most of what has previously happened is nothing but a dot on the page and can't hurt you if you won't let it. If something persists in hanging on and you deem it necessary to be fixed, *then fix it.* You don't need the *bravery of a US Marine* to mend fences and reignite friendships. Mahatma Gandhi once said, "The weak can never forgive. Forgiveness is the attribute of the strong."

So be strong! Old prejudices, unhealthy relationships and unreasonable thoughts about almost anything can now be morphed into tolerance, understanding, open mindedness and love.

No one needs anything cluttering and poisoning our mind that does not contribute to a happy life. Starting today, blame and fault are two words now discarded from your vocabulary like worthless scrap. To live happily you must operate on peace and forgiveness.

Forgiveness Does Not Change The Past But It Does Enlarge The Future.

Paul Boese

Don't leave this world with unsaid words and un-kissed lips. Saying ***I-Love-You*** is powerful. It delivers with it a wonderful feeling which is hard to replicate. ***And the best part is the deliverer of the words and the recipient of the words both share this feeling.***

By now, some of you are thinking, "Is she nuts? Why should I be the one to apologize?" Well, someone has to and why not be the bigger person. It can't hurt you and could enrich your life ***hugely***. But remember, after you do your part, the rest is up to them. Be it family or friend after trying your best to repair and restore, whether it worked or not, move on and don't look back.

Having had courage enough to take the initiative to repair the relationship you now can to live the rest of your life knowing you have done all that you can do. Oscar Wilde said, "Always forgive your enemy-nothing annoys them so much."

In The Book Of Life, The Answers Are Not In The Back.

Charlie Brown

Believe In What You Want But Do Believe

As young people, we frequently derive comfort in knowing that some supreme deity is with us at all times to guide our way and keep us safe. Our parents generally set the pattern for us by passing on their own family traditions of where, when or *even if* to worship but as we become adults many of us decide to follow our own path.

The available choices are innumerable and varied and over the years what we believe or don't believe can dramatically change. Even the strongest believers among us have had life experiences that can at some juncture cause us to become jaded, angry or questioning of the beliefs that we have responsibly carried with us our whole lives.

Of late, religious organizations are reporting declining numbers. A poll done by Harvard

Institute for Religion Research says that 40 percent attend church weekly but they **believe the numbers of those really going to church are more likely around twenty percent.**

According to a study done by the Pew Forum on Religion and Public Life, one fifth of the United States population belong to no church with six percent of us professing to be an atheist or an agnostic. **Shockingly** they found when the last census was taken, those persons checking the box indicating **no affiliation** to a particular institution or religion has **doubled since 1990**.

Religion has played such a significant role in peoples lives for centuries and has been what many of us have relied upon. So, why now this dramatic shift in our thinking? It seems some people now see organized religion as becoming more involved in war, money, power and politics and not **enough in prayer**.

The good news is sixty eight percent of persons polled did consider themselves spiritual and believed in God or a Universal Spirit and **prayed every day** even if they might not be doing it the traditional way.

I am not suggesting anyone make a mass exodus from what has been his or her religious practice. What gives a person peace and happiness is what they should be doing. I do believe that you can be dedicated to your faith even if you might not have seen the inside of a church since Sally Field was a flying nun.

Now Might Be The Time
When You Decide
To Have Faith In Your Faith.

Not being affiliated with a particular religious organization **might be leaving some of us shaking like a hooker on a cold day** but many of us have what we call a direct line to whatever we believe. That alone, at this stage of our lives, can be just what we need to give us a feeling of completeness.

Even though we may have thought our faith had let us down from time to time, having this connection can help us get through the most difficult of times.

I had a beautiful friend who died a few years ago. We were like sisters and before her illness reared it's ugly head, we did everything together. People even said we looked alike! Gail and I had numerous discussions over the years about everything including religion and we always felt free to express our own personal beliefs. As close as we were, and as similar as we were, *we did not see eye to eye about a supreme deity*.

Gail was raised in a household where believing was not given credence. She was living what she felt was a complete and happy life so at this point did not see a reason to question or change how she thought.

Enter Cancer. Did this significant life event send her running to the nearest place of prayer? No. Gail did not rush out to find faith but began the arduous battle of fighting the disease. I on the other hand began praying harder than I had ever prayed for anything in my life.

Growing up, kids pray for lots of things. I remember praying that my science teacher, Mrs. Amato would give me a good grade, for my friend AJ to teach me how to fish or for Walker, the new boy in class to think I was cute. All the sophomoric and juvenile things kids consider vital to their happiness get sent up to the heavens via prayer in hopes of being answered.

Now, my prayers were to offer Gail the strength to fight this battle and if she was not successful I prayed that she could take comfort in knowing that she would be going to a better place. However, without her having a belief system in place I wondered if this would be possible for her.

After a year and a half, sadly she lost the battle and I lost a wonderful friend. I *almost* lost something else that I find critical to my everyday happiness. My faith was now being challenged. Why did she have to die and without faith where was her soul to go? Now at an age where my faith should be my rock, my guidance, and my solace I found myself wavering. Have I wasted all my life believing?

A week or so after Gail's death I had a conversation with a lovely woman who brought me back to clear thinking. She was a neighbor who had spent a great deal of time with Gail before she died. She would look in on her often to dispense love and unknown to me at the time, prayer.

Knowing that Gail was not a believer this marvelous maven first asked her if it was all right to come to her bedside and read to her from the Bible. To my surprise, Gail had agreed. Not only did Gail listen but also during these sessions, she decided, even when it was apparent that her life would not to be spared, that *she did in fact believe*.

Faith Is The Substance Of Things Hoped For And The Evidence Of The Things Unseen.

Hebrews 11:1.

Belief in something, anything can make our day-to-day challenges more bearable and life more enjoyable. It matters less the vehicle you choose to believe with but that you put your troubles in the hands of a Higher Power. ***Whether your church is a building or a beach, don't forget to have faith!***

If your Higher Power is simply the Universe and you believe that we all have been planted here to sprout like mushrooms, that is your choice and **no one should question it.** I will personally practice optimism and continue to enjoy my direct line to *my* Higher Power feeling peace in knowing that Gail is in good hands.

Faith Is Taking The First Step Even When You Don't See The Whole Staircase

Martin Luther King, Jr.

Fifty Shades Of Advice

Life does not stop for anyone or anything. Regretfully it can be half spent before we recognize the value of what we have had. *Over the years, if you have begun to view yourself as a fossilized mess then that is how others will view you. Don't be the flower that never allowed itself to bloom.* Pessimism is a luxury no one can afford. Start each day with a smile and keep people around you that do the same. To charge your battery you have to rid yourself of those who drain it.

Wrinkles and gray hair are signs that you have lived. Young faces can be more beautiful but older faces tell a story. By the way no one can't *eat enough to fill out those wrinkles*.

So Much Has Been Said And Sung Of Beautiful Young Girls, Why Doesn't Somebody Wake Up To The Beauty Of Old Women?

Harriet Beecher Stowe

Get as much exercise as your own health condition will permit. Even when those old bones disagree with every step you take, **take them**. Exercising reduces tension, gets more air to our lungs, keeps our balance and can prevent us from moving slower than a tortoise on sedatives. Use up what God has given you.

Erma Bombeck said, "When I stand before God at the end of my life, I would hope that I would not have a single bit of talent left, and could say that I have used everything you gave me."

You don't have to be rich to have a rich life. Make your happiness happen. Brag about your age instead of mourning it. *If you are always looking for the young person you were you will never appreciate the wonderful person you are.*

The world does not always treat us the way we would like but as Dennis Wholey said, "Expecting the world to treat you fairly because you are a good person is like expecting the bull not to charge because you are a vegetarian."

In my previous book, **AGE WITH A GIGGLE,** I mentioned that showing beauty of the heart would keep your life meaningful. Reach out and show kindness to all and before you know that kindness will come back to you. Winston Churchill said, "We make a living by what we get, we make a life by what we give."

One day my grandson asked me what it was like to be old. I said it was a little difficult to explain but told him that we could do an exercise. I instructed him to go get some cotton and put it in his ears. Then I sent him for some small stones to put inside of his shoes. He then put on some safety glasses on which I had smeared Vaseline over the lenses. As he stood before me giggling, I said, "Now, that's how it feels to be old."

A Woman Has The Age She Deserves.

Coco Chanel

With the tooth fairy now leaving sympathy notes instead of money and with half of the stuff now in our shopping carts saying "For Fast Relief" we could have a lot to complain about however, **negativity will not build a happy life.** Now, I am not talking about walking around with a goofy smile on your face that could scare the cat. **I am saying find the best and give no credence to the rest.**

A lovely and wise woman, Isabel Chapman once said, "Blessed is he who expects little and receives less." If we are grateful for what we have and understanding of all that we have not, we can be the person who gives a ***new face to aging***.

None Are So Old As Those Who Have Outlived Enthusiasm.

Henry David Thoreau

CPSIA information can be obtained at www.ICGtesting.com
Printed in the USA
LVOW122223140513

333637LV00001B/3/P